Published by Ladybird Books Ltd
A Penguin Company
Penguin Books Ltd, 80 Strand, London WC2R 0RL, England
Penguin Books Australia Ltd, 250 Camberwell Road, Camberwell, Victoria 3124, Australia
Penguin Books (NZ) Ltd, Cnr Rosedale and Airborne Roads, Albany, Auckland, New Zealand

Meg and Mog Television Series copyright © Absolutely/Happy Life/Varga 2003
Based upon the books featuring the characters Meg and Mog
by Helen Nicoll and Jan Pieńkowski
Licensed by Target Entertainment
This book based on the TV episode **Meg's Treasure**
Script by Carl Gorham and Moray Hunter
Animation artwork by Roger Mainwood
First published by Ladybird Books 2004
2 4 6 8 10 9 7 5 3 1

MEG & MOG

Meg's Treasure

Ladybird

MEG & MOG
created by
Helen Nicoll and Jan Pieńkowski

It was a sunny day at the beach. Mog and Owl were fishing. Meg was watching the sea.

"Mmm, I wonder what it's like under the sea?" she thought.

It was time for a spell.

**"1, 2, 3, 4, 5,
Plummet,
Fathom,
Duck and dive!"**

There was a flash and a
thunderclap and suddenly a little
submarine was bobbing in the
water. Meg and Mog climbed
aboard straight away.

"Goodbye, Owl. We'll be back in
time for tea."

"Engines on," said Meg.

"Down periscope," said Mog.

And **dive, dive, dive!** The submarine sank into the sea. Through the window Meg and Mog saw all sorts of strange plants and creatures.

"It's so beautiful," said Meg, looking at the coral and the shells.

"Yum, yum," said Mog, as a shoal of fish swam by.

"Look!" said Meg, "A shipwreck."

There was an old ship lying on the seabed. Meg steered the submarine through a hole in its side. Then she suddenly gasped, "Treasure!"

An ancient chest was half-buried in the sand. Its lid was open and it was filled to the brim with gold coins and jewels.

Meg and Mog quickly pulled on
their diving suits and left the
submarine. They floated over to
the chest. It really was treasure.

Meg closed the lid and between
them they dragged it back inside.

But no sooner had they opened the chest again than there was a tremendous jolt.

Looking in through the window was an enormous eye – an eye belonging to a very big green person with long tentacles.

"It's a giant octopus," said Meg.
"What does he want?"

"I think he wants the treasure," said
   Mog in a quavery voice.

The giant octopus wrapped his tentacles around the submarine and gave it a good shake. Inside, Meg and Mog clung on as best they could.

It was time for another spell.

**"Terra firma,
Rock and sand,
Happy landings
On dry land!"**

With a flash and a thunderclap Meg, Mog and the treasure were back in the open air, standing on a small, solid rock. Around them stretched empty sea.

"At least it's dry," said Meg.

The giant octopus reared up out of the sea, making a huge splash.

"Well, it **was** dry," said Meg.

The octopus towered over them,
waving his tentacles.

"What does he want?" asked Meg.

One of the tentacles pointed firmly
at the treasure chest.

"I think he wants the treasure," said
Mog.

At that moment a squeaky cry seemed to come from the chest. Meg and Mog listened. The chest squeaked again. Mog lifted the lid.

The jewels and coins stirred and shifted, and a baby octopus scrambled out of the chest. The giant octopus smiled joyfully and picked the baby up with a tentacle.

"Ah," said Meg, "**that's** what he wanted."

The giant octopus hugged his baby.
Everyone was happy.

Except . . . "Er, how do we get back
to the beach?" asked Meg.

A short while later Owl, who had spent a good afternoon fishing, saw an unusual sight. A giant green octopus was swimming towards the beach and balanced on his head were Meg, Mog, a baby octopus and a treasure chest.

As they reached the shore, Meg
and Mog slid down on to the sand.
The giant octopus and his baby
waved goodbye and disappeared
under the sea.

"Here we are," said Meg.

"Fish for tea?" said Owl.

"Just perfect, Owl," said Meg.